Disney

Snow White
and the Seven Dwarfs

Disney

Snow White and the Seven Dwarfs

SCRIPT BY CECIL CASTELLUCCI

ART BY GABRIELE BAGNOLI

LETTERING BY RICHARD STARKINGS AND
COMICRAFT'S JIMMY BETANCOURT

COVER ART BY GABRIELE BAGNOLI

DARK HORSE BOOKS

DARK HORSE BOOKS

PRESIDENT AND PUBLISHER
MIKE RICHARDSON

EDITOR
FREDDYE MILLER

ASSISTANT EDITOR
JUDY KHUU

DESIGNER
BRENNAN THOME

DIGITAL ART TECHNICIAN
SAMANTHA HUMMER

DISNEY SNOW WHITE AND THE SEVEN DWARFS

Published by Dark Horse Books
A division of Dark Horse Comics LLC
10956 SE Main Street
Milwaukie, OR 97222

DarkHorse.com

To find a comics shop in your area, visit comicshoplocator.com

First edition: November 2019
ISBN 978-1-50671-462-2
Digital ISBN 978-1-50671-463-9

1 3 5 7 9 10 8 6 4 2
Printed in China

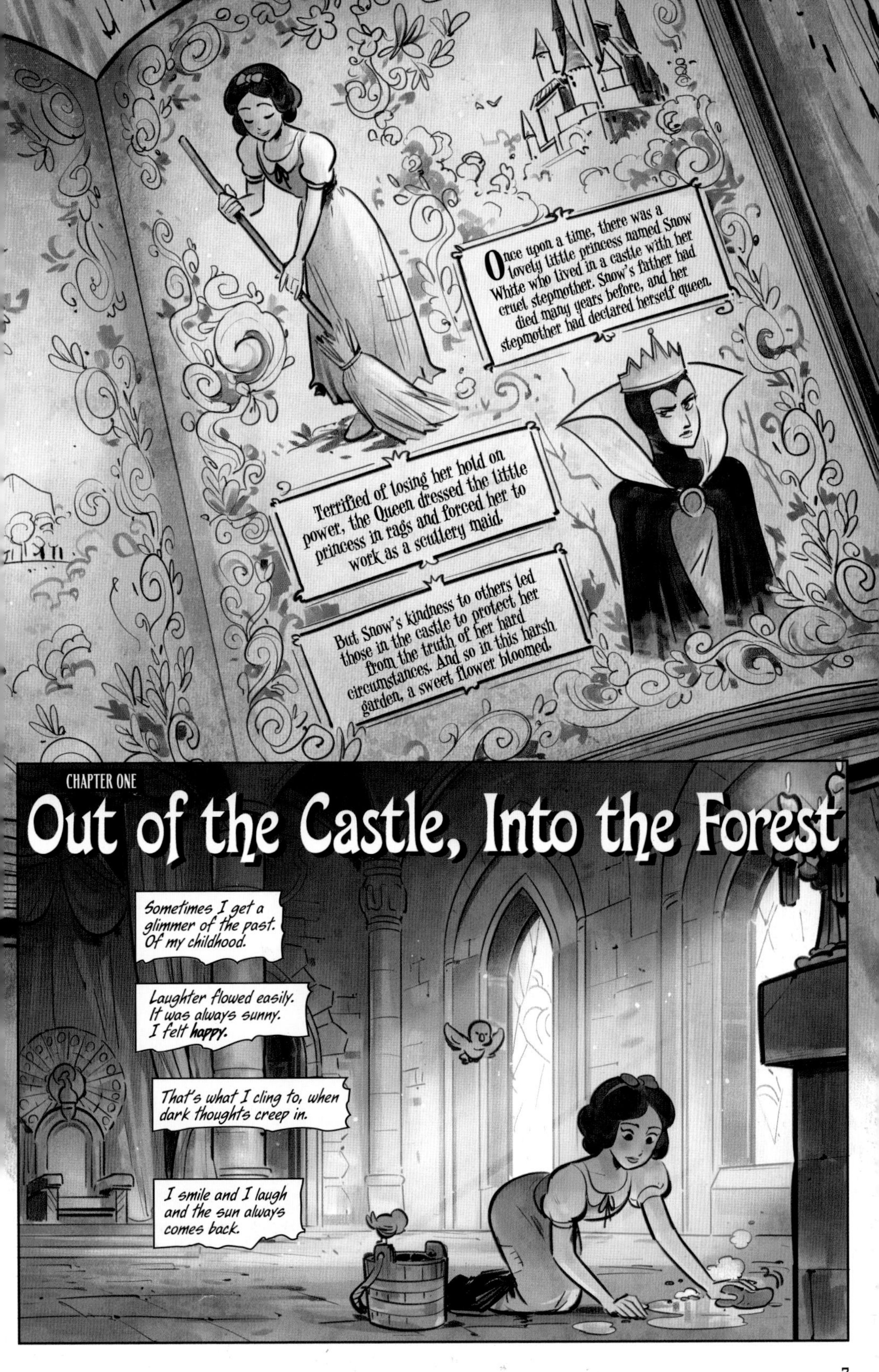
Once upon a time, there was a lovely little princess named Snow White who lived in a castle with her cruel stepmother. Snow's father had died many years before, and her stepmother had declared herself queen.
Terrified of losing her hold on power, the Queen dressed the little princess in rags and forced her to work as a scullery maid.
But Snow's kindness to others led those in the castle to protect her from the truth of her hard circumstances. And so in this harsh garden, a sweet flower bloomed.
CHAPTER ONE
Out of the Castle, Into the Forest
Sometimes I get a glimmer of the past. Of my childhood.
Laughter flowed easily. It was always sunny. I felt happy.
That's what I cling to, when dark thoughts creep in.
I smile and I laugh and the sun always comes back.

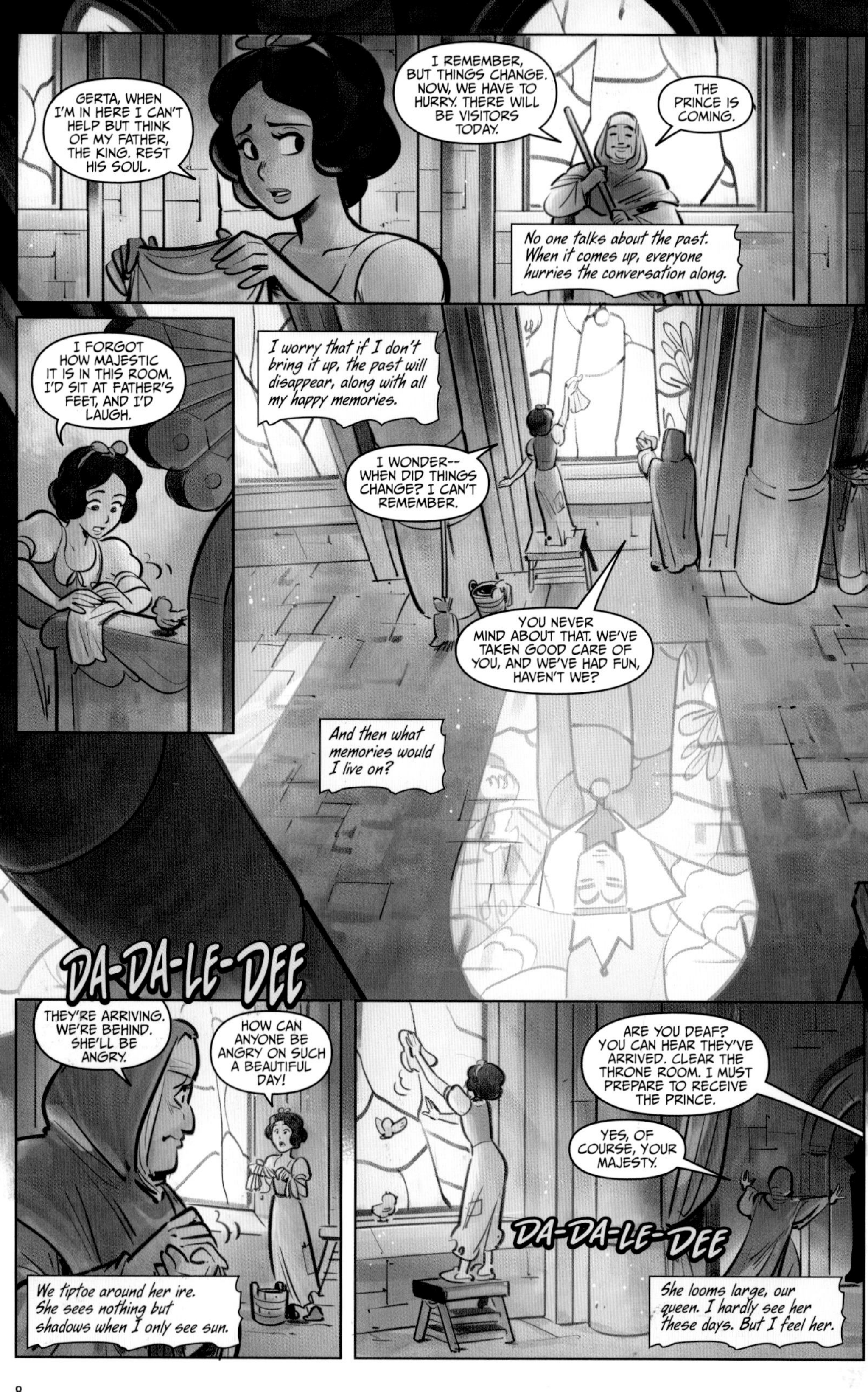
GERTA, WHEN I'M IN HERE I CAN'T HELP BUT THINK OF MY FATHER, THE KING. REST HIS SOUL.
I REMEMBER, BUT THINGS CHANGE. NOW, WE HAVE TO HURRY. THERE WILL BE VISITORS TODAY.
THE PRINCE IS COMING.
No one talks about the past. When it comes up, everyone hurries the conversation along.
I FORGOT HOW MAJESTIC IT IS IN THIS ROOM. I'D SIT AT FATHER'S FEET, AND I'D LAUGH.
I worry that if I don't bring it up, the past will disappear, along with all my happy memories.
I WONDER-- WHEN DID THINGS CHANGE? I CAN'T REMEMBER.
YOU NEVER MIND ABOUT THAT. WE'VE TAKEN GOOD CARE OF YOU, AND WE'VE HAD FUN, HAVEN'T WE?
And then what memories would I live on?
DA-DA-LE-DEE
THEY'RE ARRIVING. WE'RE BEHIND. SHE'LL BE ANGRY.
HOW CAN ANYONE BE ANGRY ON SUCH A BEAUTIFUL DAY!
We tiptoe around her ire. She sees nothing but shadows when I only see sun.
ARE YOU DEAF? YOU CAN HEAR THEY'VE ARRIVED. CLEAR THE THRONE ROOM. I MUST PREPARE TO RECEIVE THE PRINCE.
YES, OF COURSE, YOUR MAJESTY.
DA-DA-LE-DEE
She looms large, our queen. I hardly see her these days. But I feel her.

SNOW, WE HAVE TO PREPARE FOR THE PRINCE'S ARRIVAL. MAKE YOURSELF SCARCE.
BUT WE'RE NOT DONE HERE! SHE'LL WANT THE WOOD BUFFED, THE SILVER POLISHED, AND THE FIRES ROARING.
WOOP
I know what the queen likes. I remember--from when we were **family.**
I wish it were now, but that was once upon a time...
GO! GO DOWN TO THE STABLES. YOU'LL BE OUT OF THE WAY THERE.
DON'T EVER HOLD ME UP WHEN I'M ENTERING A ROOM AGAIN, OR I'LL HAVE YOUR HEAD.
YES, YOUR MAJESTY.
It hurts that the castle staff are always sending me out of rooms.
THANK YOU, FRIENDS. IT'S BEEN SO LONG SINCE THE CASTLE HAS HAD GUESTS. I SUPPOSE A PRINCE VISITING IS AN OCCASION.
But Gerta and the others have always known best.
IMAGINE. A REAL LIVE PRINCE! I WONDER IF I'LL GET TO STEAL A LOOK AT HIM!
They have taught me to always look for the light when there is darkness.
The light is always there. Shining.

SNOW! SHOULD YOU BE HERE? I THOUGHT YOU WERE IN THE KITCHENS?
GERTA SENT ME HERE TO HELP WITH THE HORSES.
The huntsman has always clucked over me like a dear friend.
WELL, GERTA KNOWS BEST. THE PRINCE MAY WANT TO HUNT, AND WE MUST BE READY.
ARE YOU HUNTING TODAY? I CAN TAKE OVER HERE IF YOU WANT TO ATTEND TO THE ARMORY.
When you grow up alone, you are grateful for the care that people show you.
I always try to be helpful to show my appreciation for what they've taught me.
YOU ARE SWEETNESS AND LIGHT, SNOW.
IT'S NO TROUBLE AT ALL. I LOVE ANIMALS, AND THEY LOVE ME.
The animals are my friends, too. It's a kind of magic, the way they always gather around me.
No task ever seems too hard or dreary with them around.
WHY, HELLO. WE WERE TOLD TO STABLE OUR HORSES HERE.
WHAT A BEAUTIFUL HORSE.
HE'S A FINE STEED, IT'S TRUE. FAST. BRIGHT. RIDES WITH HEART.
The steed shows the man. This man is good. How kind of him to make sure the prince's horse is taken care of.

HE FEELS LIKE AN OLD FRIEND TO ME.
HE'S TAKEN WITH YOU. USUALLY HE'S SHY AND SKITTISH AROUND STRANGERS.
I don't have the opportunity to meet that many new people, but here I am, completely at ease.
AS AM I. BUT I SUPPOSE SOMETIMES YOU MEET SOMEONE, AND YOU'RE KINDRED SPIRITS RIGHT AWAY.
IT'S HARD TO CUT TO THE CORE OF A PERSON. WE WEAR SUCH MASKS MOST OF THE TIME.
Something is happening here. I feel at home with him in a way I never have before.
I DON'T LIKE MASKS. OR SHADOWS. I TRY TO BE IN THE LIGHT.
I AM MOST MYSELF WHEN I'M ALONE.
I look into this stranger's eyes, and I seem to know him as though he were already a part of myself.
YES. OUTSIDE OF THE CASTLE, IN THE GARDEN OR THE STABLE, I ALWAYS FEEL I CAN BE MYSELF.
As though I have already known him for a long time.
Always find the light, I say. Here it is, a spark right in front of me.

HAVE YOU HAD HIM LONG? DO YOU SHOW HIM?
A FEW YEARS NOW. TRUTH BE TOLD, HE'S THE BOSS OF ME. HE MASTERS ME MORE THAN I MASTER HIM.
This moment started so small, but I can feel it blooming into something astonishing.
Seconds linger and turn into minutes.
I SEE YOUR STRATEGY HERE. CLEVER GIRL. YOU'VE BEATEN ME AGAIN.
MY FATHER TAUGHT ME. HE WAS BRILLIANT AT GAMES AND BATTLE.
Minutes turn into an hour.
YOU'RE KIND TO HELP ME. IT'S THE ROOT VEGETABLES THAT ARE THE HARDEST TO DIG OUT.
IT'S SUCH A CHANGE FROM MY NORMAL DUTIES THAT IT'S A PLEASURE. AND YOU'VE PROMISED ME A PICNIC.
We are both hungry for food, for life, for conversation.
THIS IS MY FAVORITE SPOT IN THE WHOLE CASTLE. THERE'S A WHOLE WORLD OUT THERE. ISN'T THAT WONDERFUL?
YES. BUT I FEEL AS THOUGH I'VE FOUND THAT A WHOLE WORLD LIVES WITHIN THIS CASTLE GARDEN.
I want to share my secrets with him. it feels natural.
I want to kiss him. I've never felt this before.

HAVE YOU ALWAYS WORKED IN THE CASTLE?
YES. I'VE LIVED HERE MY WHOLE LIFE.
I like the way he looks at me. As if I were me, and not the poor little princess.

HAVE YOU ALWAYS WORKED FOR THE PRINCE?
IN A FASHION. YES.
I will have to tell him the truth. But for now, it's my secret to keep.

I WISH MY CIRCUMSTANCES WERE DIFFERENT.
I wish that, too.
I feel as though time has stopped just for us.

Today the colors sing. The future feels bright.

THERE YOU ARE. WE'VE BEEN LOOKING FOR YOU. WE'LL BE LATE.
And just like that, the moment's over.

I LOST TRACK OF TIME. I WAS TOO BUSY TALKING WITH...
OH, MY. I'D BETTER GET BACK TO THE KITCHEN TO HELP PREPARE THE DINNER.
But there is a promise of more to come.

WHY, I DON'T EVEN KNOW YOUR NAME!
NOR DO I KNOW YOURS!
And isn't it a wonder that the regular can be interrupted by the extraordinary?

I wish this moment could last. With him. Forever.

DUTY CALLS. BUT WILL YOU MEET ME LATER, NEW FRIEND? AND TELL ME YOUR NAME THEN?
THAT GIVES US SOMETHING TO LOOK FORWARD TO UPON OUR REUNION.
Just a few more hours before I can get to know him better.

SNOW! I'LL BE NEEDING YOU IN THE KITCHEN!
This must be a dream...I hope it's not. But if so, I will hold on to it forever.

WHERE IS EVERYONE? THEY MUST BE BUSY WITH THE PRINCE.
THIS MUST BE THE QUEEN'S LUNCH. SHE WON'T WANT IT COLD. I'LL BRING IT TO HER AND SAVE DEAR GERTA A TRIP.
When a heart is full, it's good to pass on the joy to someone else!
And the Queen has cared for me all these years.

HELLO? QUEEN MOTHER? I'VE BROUGHT YOUR LUNCH!
Why am I trembling?
OH, THIS ROOM IS COLD.
It could use a fire.
I KNOW QUEEN MOTHER HATES TO HAVE A CHILL.
I've seen her rage when the fire goes out.
AND I WILL DO ANYTHING TO BRING HER A LITTLE HAPPINESS.

I tell myself that people express love differently.

THERE. THE FIRE IS ROARING. I FEEL COZIER. IT'S ALWAYS BEST TO LOOK FOR A WAY TO SOLVE YOUR OWN TROUBLES.

OH. MY HANDS ARE DIRTY. THAT WON'T DO. QUEEN MOTHER ALWAYS SAYS THAT A GIRL SHOULD KEEP CLEAN.

She shows her care in her rigid rules--for the castle, for the land, for me. That's what makes her an iron queen.

MY, MY, I AM A FRIGHT!

I feel I can see deeply inside of my own self...
SNOW WHITE. WHAT ARE YOU DOING IN MY INNER CHAMBER?
I BROUGHT YOUR LUNCH. I THOUGHT YOU MIGHT WANT TO EAT BEFORE YOUR MEETING WITH THE PRINCE.
THERE'S NEVER ANY TIME TO EAT WHEN YOU MIX, YOU ALWAYS SAY. AND I MADE A FIRE TO WARM YOU.
I tremble at her power. I want her love.
She has mine.

HOW CONSIDERATE. YOU REALLY DO HAVE A HEART, DON'T YOU, SNOW?
She noticed!
LET ME LOOK AT YOU. I HAVEN'T SEEN YOU IN AN AGE.
I wish I were wearing my good dress.
NOW THAT YOU'RE OLDER, WE'LL HAVE TO DO SOMETHING ABOUT YOU. WON'T WE? BUT THAT IS FOR LATER. TODAY YOU MUST REMAIN OUT OF SIGHT.
OH, YES. PERHAPS I COULD TAKE ON OTHER DUTIES! I'D LOVE TO LEARN MORE ABOUT CARING FOR THE ANIMALS!
GERTA. I CAN'T HAVE MY GUESTS BEING INTRUDED UPON. SEE THAT SHE STAYS IN HER PLACE.
Perhaps I am old enough now to move on to different duties.
OF COURSE, YOUR HIGHNESS. APOLOGIES. COME, SNOW.
Our meetings never quite go the way I'd hoped.

STAY HERE AND DRAW FROM THE WELL. WITH SO MANY GUESTS, WE ALWAYS NEED MORE WATER. THAT WILL BE YOUR JOB.

OF COURSE. BUT I DO WISH I COULD STEAL A GLANCE AT THE PRINCE.

I can hear the castle coming to life. With conversation and music. It lifts my spirits.

ONE DAY YOU WILL GO TO MANY DANCES AND SEE MANY PRINCES. BUT NOT TODAY. YOU ***MUST*** STAY IN THE GARDEN.

I want that to be true. I want to see it all. I want to be there, now.

SOME SAY YOU CAN WISH AT A WELL FOR YOUR HEART'S DESIRE.

I wish, wish, wish, with all my heart, that I could be a bird to peek inside and gaze at all the guests.
No, I wish that I could see him soon. That we'd dance in the ballroom.

I WISH THAT HE'D COME HERE NOW AND FIND ME.
FIND ME.

⸗SIGH⸗ SILLY SNOW. HOW WILL HE FIND YOU IF YOU'RE HERE IN THE GARDEN, AND HE'S WORKING IN THE CASTLE? I'LL HAVE TO WISH HARDER.
WISH HARDER.
HELLO. I'VE BEEN LOOKING FOR YOU.
YOU'RE HERE! OH!
Sometimes when a wish is answered, it startles.
I HAVE TO TELL YOU. I HAVE TO SPEAK FROM MY HEART. I MUST CONFESS.
CONFESS?
Does he know my secret? Am I discovered?
I AM THE PRINCE.
I'M SORRY. I DIDN'T MEAN TO FRIGHTEN YOU. DON'T RUN AWAY. I HAVE SO MUCH THAT I WANT TO SAY.

YOU MEAN YOU ARE THE PRINCE? HIMSELF?
YES.
I WASN'T STRAIGHT WITH YOU WHEN WE MET. I WANTED TO KEEP UP THE CHARADE.
What kind of dream is this?

AND YOU'VE ENCHANTED ME. I WANT TO KNOW YOU MORE.

SO DO I. AND I HAVE MUCH TO TELL YOU, TOO. BUT NOT HERE, NOT NOW.
I WANT TO HEAR IT ALL. I WANT TO TELL YOU ALL.
This day. This perfectly wonderful day that brought him here to me.

LET ME MAKE MYSELF PRESENTABLE, WON'T YOU?
IF YOU MUST. BUT I TAKE YOU AS YOU ARE. I HAVE SOME BUSINESS TO TAKE CARE OF UNTIL WE MEET AGAIN.
So this is joy. I never thought I could feel it. It seemed so removed. But here it is, and it suits me well.

UNTIL THEN. WE HAVE FOREVER IN FRONT OF US, DON'T WE?
WE DO. A WHOLE LIFE. OUR TWO HEARTS TOGETHER.
This is the light.

THERE YOU ARE. GET OUT OF THOSE RAGS. WE'LL HAVE TO MAKE QUICK WORK OF IT.
OF WHAT?
The dress! Are all my wishes coming true?
YOU'RE TO GO OUTSIDE OF THE CASTLE ON A SMALL ERRAND. THE QUEEN COMMANDS IT AND WANTS YOU TO WEAR THIS, AS YOU'LL BE REPRESENTING THE LAND.
DO YOU THINK SHE'LL LET ME WEAR IT A LITTLE LONGER WHEN I RETURN?
I could meet him in this. It would be perfect.
IF YOU DO THE ERRAND WELL, SHE MIGHT SEE IT IN HER HEART TO LET YOU.
THEN I WILL BE SURE TO EXCEED THE QUEEN'S EXPECTATIONS.
First I will finish my tasks, and then, when I meet the prince again, I will reveal myself.
THEY WOULD HAVE BEEN PROUD OF THE LADY YOU'VE BECOME. WE ALL SAW TO THAT.
THANK YOU.
Now that my heart is twinned, I feel that my love for everyone is deepening.
YOU LOOK SO MUCH LIKE YOUR MOTHER AND FATHER. I CAN SEE ALL OF THEIR NOBLE DEEDS STILL LIVE INSIDE OF YOU.
I WISH I'D KNOWN THEM LONGER.

IF YOU LIKE, YOU COULD PICK SOME WILDFLOWERS. I KNOW THAT'S SOMETHING YOU ENJOY.

YES. THAT WOULD BE LOVELY. NOTHING LIFTS A SPIRIT LIKE WILDFLOWERS. BUT TELL ME, WHAT IS MY TASK TODAY IN TOWN?

I can wear some flowers in my hair when I meet my prince again.

IS IT DIPLOMACY? WHAT DO THE PEOPLE NEED FROM ME? AM I UP TO THE CHALLENGE?

We'll talk, and we'll make plans to be together.

HELLO THERE, LITTLE ONE. ARE YOU LOST?

TWEET!

TWEET!

We will seal it with a kiss.

GOODBYE!
All can be right in the world with a little help.
AAAAH!
And then, just like that, my world is changed again.
I CAN'T DO IT. FORGIVE ME.
BUT I DON'T UNDERSTAND.
It's cruel that happiness can leave as quickly as it arrived.
All my best-laid plans wash away in this moment.
THE QUEEN. SHE'S MAD. SHE'S JEALOUS OF YOU. SHE WANTS YOU DEAD. RUN AWAY.
And what you always thought of as love shows itself to be hate.
RUN!
My whole world is torn away.

RUN AWAY AND DON'T EVER COME BACK, YOUR HIGHNESS!
How can you know where to go when the world makes no sense anymore?
What place is safe when there is only danger?
How can one find the light in such darkness?

Life as I know it seems over.
All I can do is run. I run. I run.
The shadows are alive! They're reaching for me!
Where to go? Is there anywhere in the world that is safe?

CHAPTER TWO

Home is Where the Heart is

Where am I going? Nowhere. There is nowhere to go.
This horror is going on forever.

What is that? Is that her? Is she coming? Is she here?
How can she hate me so much? What did I ever do?
Keep running. Keep moving. Don't stop. Don't ever stop.

There is no light. There are monsters everywhere.

My mind is reeling.
This must be a nightmare. This can't be real! Oh, but it is. What is that watching me?

How can I possibly bear it if it's true?
I can't go on. I can't.
I feel so utterly alone.
I realize now I've been alone my whole life.
Is there any good to be found in the world?
OHHHHHHHH!

OH! I'M SORRY. THIS HAS BEEN A TERRIBLE DAY. YOU'RE JUST TRYING TO HELP ME. PLEASE DON'T RUN AWAY.

I'VE BEEN SO AFRAID. I DON'T KNOW WHAT TO DO NOW THAT MY WHOLE WORLD HAS GONE WRONG. DO YOU KNOW WHAT THAT'S LIKE?

TWEET TWEET!

TWEET!

TWEET!

YOU DO KNOW. I SUPPOSE I COULD BE LIKE YOU AND SING A SONG. THAT ALWAYS LIFTS MY HEART.

CHEEP!

TWEET!

TWEET!

CHEEP!

LISTENING TO YOU, I FEEL BETTER ALREADY! A SONG IS ALL I NEED TO SEE THE LIGHT IN THIS TERRIBLE PLACE.

IT'S GETTING LATE. AND I DO NEED A PLACE TO SLEEP.

WHY, IT'S CHARMING. IT'S JUST THE PERFECT PLACE. IT'S SO SMALL AND SWEET.
Do I dare believe my eyes or listen to my heart?
I trusted the Queen my whole life and look where it led me.
I have no other choice but to hope for the best.
Not everyone is bad.
IT'S NOT VERY WELL KEPT. LOOK AT THAT MESS OF A GARDEN. AND THE WINDOWS! SO DIRTY. THAT ROOF! OH, I SHOULDN'T JUDGE.
TWEET!
HOW DO I LOOK? PRESENTABLE?
I HOPE THEY'LL WELCOME ME.
KNOCK KNOCK KNOCK
IT'S QUIET. NO ONE'S HOME.
HELLO? HELLO? MAY I COME IN?
SQUEEEEEEEEAK

WHY, LOOK AT THIS PLACE. IT'S WELL LIVED IN, BUT WHAT A MESS!
I don't know. Perhaps I should leave. It all seems strange.
SEVEN LITTLE CHAIRS. SEVEN LITTLE PLATES. SEVEN LITTLE CUPS. MUST BE SEVEN CHILDREN. MESSY CHILDREN.
I've always believed that something can be more than what it seems.
First impressions aren't necessarily true.
THIS FIREPLACE IS A HAZARD. THIS STEW LOOKS LIKE GRUEL. THE DISHES AREN'T DONE.
I need to look beyond what I see.
COBWEBS EVERYWHERE. SO MANY THINGS NEED FIXING. IT'S NOT VERY CHEERY. BUT IT COULD BE.
A little hard work and tender care can change your perspective about any place!
Remember, a diamond doesn't look beautiful until it's polished!
And like the Queen, the most beautiful diamond can cut the deepest.
I can't live in fear. I must make a plan for the best.
MAYBE THEY HAVE NO ONE TO LOOK AFTER THEM. I'LL TIDY UP TO SURPRISE THEM, AND PERHAPS THEY WILL LET ME STAY.

YOU TAKE THE TABLE. YOU TAKE THE DISHES. YOU DUST THE SHELVES. I'LL SWEEP THE ROOM.

THERE. NOW. A GOOD SUPPER WILL MAKE THIS PICTURE COMPLETE.

WITH A LITTLE LOVE, THIS GARDEN COULD BLOOM.
Action helps clear the cobwebs of the mind.
I wouldn't want to take advantage of any kindness!

I'LL NEED TO CONVINCE THEM I HAVE SKILLS TO OFFER TO PAY FOR THE ROOF OVER MY HEAD.
I'm still worried about my future, but I feel calmer already.

I HOPE THEY LIKE WHAT I'VE DONE AND WILL LET ME STAY.
A fire and the smell of simmering stew soothes even the most ravaged soul.

MAYBE I'LL REST FOR A MOMENT WHILE I WAIT FOR THE CHILDREN TO COME HOME AND FOR SUPPER TO COOK.
The warmth gets into every nook and cranny and drives the fear away.

I THINK EVERYTHING IS GOING TO BE FINE.
WHY, LOOK HOW SMALL THE BEDS ARE! AND THEY ALL HAVE NAMES ON THEM. WHAT FUNNY NAMES!
DOPEY
SNEEZY
I HOPE THEY DON'T MIND. I'M TOO BIG OTHERWISE!
DOPEY
LET ME DREAM OF LOVELY THINGS AND FORGET ABOUT THE HORROR OF THIS DAY!
My heart feels warm. I can't explain why, but I feel safe.
SNEEZY
HAPPY
I have done all I can do. Rest now.

WHO'S THAT?
I WISH THAT HADN'T BEEN ALL A DREAM.
Where am I again? Everything here is so small and unfamiliar. It's the little house.
IS IT A GHOST?
OR A DEMON?
WHY, IT'S A GIRL!
SHE LOOKS LIKE TROUBLE.
OH, GRUMPY.
OH!

WHY, YOU'RE NOT CHILDREN.

YOU'RE LITTLE MEN!

OF COURSE WE'RE NOT CHILDREN.
WHO ARE YOU CALLING LITTLE? I'M EXACTLY THE SIZE I'M SUPPOSED TO BE.
TALL, REALLY, FOR OUR KIND.
ATCHOO!
I've always been able to see kindness in the strangers I meet.

YOU'RE RIGHT. I'M SORRY. I KNOW OUR LANDS HOUSE MANY KINDS.
I hope that they can see the goodness in me.

I STILL HAVE SO MUCH TO LEARN. CAN YOU FORGIVE ME? CAN WE START AGAIN?
OH, SHE'S SWEET.
BUT WHO IS SHE?
YES. WHO ARE YOU?
TROUBLE, THAT'S WHAT SHE IS. MARK MY WORDS.
I call on all I learned as a princess. Sit up straight. Exude kindness. Always listen. Know others as you know yourself.

I BET I CAN GUESS WHO YOU ALL ARE. BASHFUL, SNEEZY, DOPEY, DOC, HAPPY, SLEEPY...AND YOU MUST BE GRUMPY.

WHY, YES! YOU GOT US ALL RIGHT!

IT'S SO NICE TO MEET YOU AND TO BE IN YOUR COZY HOME. I AM SNOW WHITE!

THE PRINCESS?
BUT WHAT IS SHE DOING HERE?
LEAVING, I HOPE.

I'M IN HIDING. WON'T YOU HELP ME? THE QUEEN WANTS TO KILL ME.
It's hard to think of my stepmother in this new way. I both love and fear her.

I CAN'T GO BACK TO THE CASTLE. I MUST HIDE.
I'M HOPING THAT YOU'LL SEE IT IN YOUR HEARTS TO LET ME STAY.

TROUBLE, I TELL YOU. TROUBLE.
NOW, WE ALL KNOW THAT THE QUEEN IS EVIL. SHE'S TERRIBLE.
WHY, I'M ALLERGIC TO HER.
SHE GIVES ME NIGHTMARES.
I ALWAYS HIDE... WHEN I HEAR HER... NAME.
BUT SHOULDN'T WE HELP SOMEONE IN DISTRESS?

I WON'T BE A BURDEN. I CAN TAKE CARE OF MYSELF. I CAN BE OF HELP WITH CHORES AROUND THE HOUSE. LIKE... SUPPER?
WHY, IS THAT WHAT THAT SMELL IS? DELICIOUS.
IT SMELLS READY. *ATCHOOO!*
HOW DO WE KNOW YOU'RE NOT EVIL LIKE THE QUEEN? THAT YOU WON'T POISON US?

I WOULD NEVER.
I had no idea others saw the Queen in this way.

IT DOES SMELL GOOD.
I'M ALWAYS SLEEPY BEFORE I'M HUNGRY.
I'D RATHER STARVE.
I'LL BE GLAD TO TASTE IT.
I HOPE THERE IS NO PEPPER.
I'LL BRAVE IT--IT SMELLS SO GOOD.

I'LL GET IT READY WHILE YOU ALL WASH UP.
WASH UP!!!!
I TOLD YOU SHE WAS TROUBLE.

SO, WE USE THE SOAP?
AND THE WATER. SCOOP IT UP AND MAKE A LATHER.
I'M ALLERGIC TO WASHING.
SHE CAN'T STAY HERE. WHAT IF THE QUEEN COMES A-LOOKING? THAT COULD BRING TROUBLE ON OUR HOUSE.
WE DON'T WANT THAT.
SPLASH
THE QUEEN IS EVIL. TERRIBLE. WICKED.
WHY DOES SHE HAVE TO BE OUR PROBLEM? WE HAVE TO BE SMART.
WELL, SHE'S ALREADY HERE. SHE HAS ALREADY COOKED.
THAT SETTLES IT. SHE STAYS THE NIGHT. ONE NIGHT.
SPLASH
ATCHOO!
SPLASH
I can change my fate, turn it around into something new.
ONE NIGHT. WELL, IT'S BETTER THAN NOTHING, BUT I CAN'T GO BACK TO THE WOODS INDEFINITELY. I'VE JUST GOT TO TRY TO CONVINCE THEM TO LET ME STAY AT LEAST UNTIL I CAN MAKE A PLAN.
I like this house, these people. I feel like myself here. And they feel like new old friends.

I have to pause and say thanks for the warmth of the room. The roof above.
Thank you for the warmth. Thank you for the roof. Thank you for the food. Thank you for the chance...
And I have to marvel at how the strange so quickly becomes the familiar.
WHY, THAT WAS DELICIOUS.
CAN I HAVE SECONDS?
I'M FULL AS FULL CAN BE.
ATCHOO!
I SUPPOSE WE'RE NOT DEAD YET.
Each one of them wears his heart on his sleeve in a different way.
WE WERE SO BUSY EATING, WE DIDN'T GET A CHANCE TO TALK.
NOW, YOU SAY YOU HAVE TALENTS. WHAT ELSE CAN YOU COOK? APPLE DUMPLINGS?
PIES?
Simple pleasures are important. I know that, having had to make do with the simplest of things at the castle.
ALL KINDS OF PIES! GOOSEBERRY PIES! AND I CAN FIX THINGS AND TEND THE GARDEN. YOU'LL SEE--I CAN BE OF GREAT USE.
They are rustic. And raw. And not what I am used to. But somehow, I like them very much.

NOW, WE INSIST. YOU TAKE THE UPSTAIRS.
I DON'T WANT TO CAUSE ANY MORE TROUBLE THAN I ALREADY HAVE. I CAN SLEEP DOWN HERE.
THAT WOULDN'T DO. WE'D BE UNHAPPY.
NOT ME. I WANT MY BED.
IT'S JUST ONE NIGHT.
Just one night. But tomorrow I have to face the nightmare...
GOOD NIGHT. AND THANK YOU.
Oh, that I could find some answers and make sense of this madness!
BLESS THE SEVEN LITTLE MEN WHO HAVE BEEN SO KIND TO ME. AND...AND MAY MY DREAMS COME TRUE. AMEN.
OH, YES! AND PLEASE MAKE GRUMPY LIKE ME.

THANK YOU FOR LETTING ME STAY THE NIGHT.
BREAKFAST WAS... FINE.
AND I'M AMAZED I WAS AWAKE ON TIME.
NOW, WE HAVE ONE RULE. DON'T LET ANYONE IN WHILE WE'RE AT WORK.
SO I CAN STAY?
WE'D BE HAPPY TO HAVE YOU FOR ONE MORE DAY.
ONE MORE DAY.

WELL, THAT WON'T DO.
SQUEEEEEEEEAK
SQUEEK

HANG YOUR HATS, FRIENDS. WIPE YOUR FEET. WASH YOUR HANDS. IT'S TIME FOR TREATS.
I SMELL GOOSEBERRY PIE!
Everything feels just right.
WILL YOU LOOK AT THAT?
HEY, THE DOOR DOESN'T SQUEAK.
SHE'S VERY THOUGHTFUL.
SLEEPY
DOC
DOPEY
HAPPY
THINGS FEEL DIFFERENT. AWAKE.
NO DUST MEANS I CAN BREATHE.
THIS IS JUST MORE OF HER WILES. MARK MY WORDS--THE QUEEN WILL FIND HER AND WREAK HER VENGEANCE!
WELL, SINCE YOU'VE MADE SUPPER, YOU MIGHT AS WELL STAY ANOTHER WEEK.
WHY, THANK YOU, DOC. I'D BE DELIGHTED.
I WAS HOPING I COULD STAY AT LEAST UNTIL I FINISH SOME OF THE PROJECTS I'VE STARTED. THE ROOF, THE FLOOR, THE WALLS, THE GARDEN...
THAT MAKES SENSE TO ME.
SWOON
GIVE A PERSON AN INCH, AND THEY TAKE A MILE.
SPEAK FOR YOURSELF.

And just like that...
NOW, DON'T LET ANYBODY IN.
I WON'T.

Every day is blissfully the same.
TING
TING

DON'T LET ANYBODY IN.
I WON'T.

DON'T LET ANYBODY IN.
I WON'T.
The days have turned into weeks.

DON'T LET ANYONE IN...

The weeks have turned into a whole month.
And I feel right at home.
I don't think anything could ever take my enormous happiness away.

CHAPTER THREE
Delicious Poison, Sweet End.
Every day I'm here, my worries seem to move farther away.
After such uncertainty, there is joy in my life again.
I have found my place among these new friends.
IT SOUNDS WONDERFUL! YOU'RE ALL VERY TALENTED!
There is warmth.
There is music.

I THINK IT'S BEEN YEARS SINCE WE'VE PLAYED.
I'M JUST SO HAPPY!
As the weeks have gone by, my old life at the castle has started to feel like a dream.

THE PIANO IS STILL A LITTLE OUT OF TUNE.
BUT IT SOUNDS FINE FOR OUR PARTY TONIGHT. WE CAN GET THAT FIXED FOR NEXT TIME.

TING TING
It's a different life than I've known...

...but it's a good one.

MAY I?

YOU MAY!

It's livelier.

At the castle, I often used to dream of going to dances one day.
I imagined the pomp and glamour.

But I never dreamt of a dance like this one.

The only thing missing from this moment is my prince.

I wonder if I will ever see him again?
I hope I do. I wish.

ALL THAT DANCING! I'M SO TIRED. AND IT'S ALMOST TIME FOR BED.

OH, THAT'S SAD. MAYBE TELL US A HAPPY STORY?

ONCE THERE WAS A PRINCESS...
WAS THE PRINCESS YOU?
WE'D LIKE TO GET TO KNOW YOU MORE.

AND SHE MET A PRINCE! AND SHE FELL IN LOVE.

WHAT WAS THE PRINCE LIKE?
WHAT DID HE DO TO WIN YOUR LOVE?

FALLING IN LOVE WAS QUITE EASY!
HE COULD CALM A HORSE WITH THE SWEEP OF HIS HAND. PLAY A SKILLED GAME OF STONES AND STICKS.
BUT MORE THAN THAT, HE LISTENED TO ME AND WAS... WONDERFUL.

DID HE SAY HE LOVED YOU?
DID HE ASK FOR A KISS?
IF HE HAD ASKED FOR ONE, I WOULD HAVE SAID YES.
THAT SOMEDAY WE'D MEET AGAIN.
YOU ALL KNOW I'M HAPPY HERE WITH YOU, BUT SOMETIMES I WISH MY PRINCE WOULD COME.
THERE ARE SO MANY THINGS I WANT TO SAY TO HIM. SO MANY ADVENTURES I WANT TO HAVE WITH HIM.

WE DON'T WANT YOU TO LEAVE. YOU BRIGHTEN OUR DAY WITH FRESH FLOWERS AND DELICIOUS PIES!
I SLEEP BETTER SINCE YOU'VE BEEN HERE. OR AT LEAST, I CAN STAY AWAKE SOME.
...
I DON'T SNEEZE AS MUCH WITH YOU AROUND.
NO SUCH THING AS A GOOD THING THAT LASTS FOREVER. SOMETHING ALWAYS HAPPENS TO SNATCH IT AWAY.
WE HOPE YOU SEE YOUR PRINCE AGAIN ONE DAY.
BUT YOU ARE ALWAYS WELCOME HERE.
It's a silly wish to try to find him. I must keep safe.
The Queen hates me and wants me dead. How could I go and look for him when I know I'm safe here?
GOOD NIGHT. YOU ALL MEAN THE WORLD TO ME.

NOW, DON'T FORGET.
I WON'T FORGET, DOC: TALK TO NO ONE.
Time passes by. Danger, when not a constant companion, recedes to memory.

NOT A SOUL IS TO COME INTO OUR HOUSE.
I'M SAFE, GRUMPY. NO ONE EVER COMES HERE. WE'RE QUITE ALONE IN THESE WOODS.
HARRUMPH. CAN'T BE TOO CAREFUL.
So perhaps by now the Queen has forgotten all about me.

ANOTHER FULL DAY IN FRONT OF ME. WHERE SHOULD I BEGIN?
Or if not, perhaps she's no longer looking for me.

TWEET! TWEET!
WHAT'S THAT? THE BERRIES HAVE COME IN? WELL THEN, I KNOW JUST WHAT TO DO!

Daily tasks here are never a chore.

Every day makes me feel a little stronger. Like I'm starting to feel safe.
It's a quiet life, but a full one.
ALL ALONE, MY PET?
OH! YOU STARTLED ME.
A stranger. I've never seen a soul around here.
MAKING PIES, I SEE. IT'S APPLE PIES THAT MAKES THE MENFOLK'S MOUTHS WATER.

THE LITTLE MEN NOT HERE?
She must be a friend of theirs if she knows who lives here.
I'M MAKING PIES FOR THEIR RETURN.
I confess it is nice to talk to someone. It's hard to be alone all day.
NOTHING BETTER THAN AN APPLE PIE.
THEY DO LOOK DELICIOUS.
WAIT TILL YOU TASTE IT.
LIKE TO TRY ONE?

AIEEEEEEE!
She's in danger.
HELP!
I know they told me to keep the door closed, but I must help her.
SHOO! SHOO, I SAY!

OH, MY HEART. QUICK--TAKE ME INTO THE HOUSE, GIRL.

I know I shouldn't, but she's winded. She needs help.

What harm could it do to give her sanctuary? She's only an old woman who has had a fright.
Surely it will be fine for her to rest for a moment. And then I'll make her leave, straightaway.

I'M SORRY IF THEY SCARED YOU.

YOU'RE SO KIND, YOUNG LADY.

THEY'RE USUALLY SO HELPFUL. I DON'T KNOW WHAT'S GOTTEN INTO THEM TODAY.

SO KIND THAT I'LL SHARE A SECRET WITH YOU.

THIS IS A *WISHING* APPLE.

A WISHING APPLE?
ONE BITE, AND ALL YOUR DREAMS COME TRUE.
NOW. MAKE A WISH AND TAKE A BITE.
THERE ARE SO MANY THINGS THAT I SHOULD WISH FOR.

THEN HURRY UP. DON'T LET THE WISH GROW COLD.

I WISH. I WISH.
That my prince will come.

OH, I FEEL STRANGE.

Stepmother? I can feel your presence.

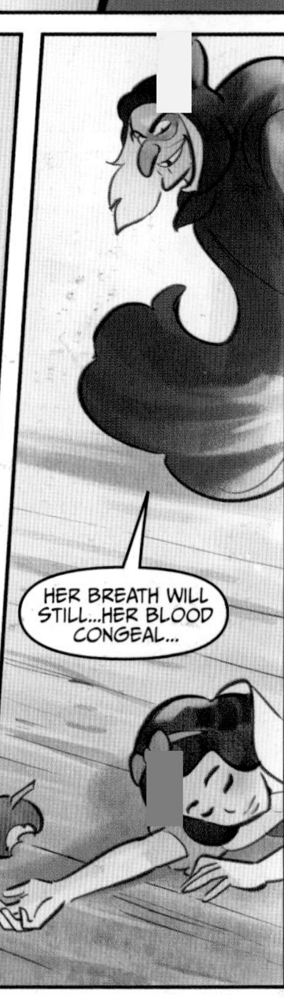
HER BREATH WILL STILL...HER BLOOD CONGEAL...

NOW I'LL BE THE FAIREST IN THE LAND!
I can't see you, but...it **is** you, stepmother.
This is a dream.

IT IS DONE!
What did I ever do to you?
HA HA HA HA HA HA
I can feel your wrath, stepmother, but I have always loved and admired you.

WHAT'S THIS? GET AWAY FROM ME YOU WRETCHED BIRDS.
Tell me what I've done to make you feel as you do!
Help! She's getting away.
Someone's coming. I hear hooves.

THERE SHE GOES.
SHE'S HEADING UP THE MOUNTAIN!
DON'T LET HER GET AWAY!
Oh, my friends. You were warning me. Why didn't I listen?
I'm sorry I didn't heed your advice and I let someone in.
I DON'T KNOW WHAT'S HAPPENED TO HER... BUT SHE'S GONE.
If only you could hear me. I'm not dead. I must be asleep. This is a dream.
WE RAN HER OUT OF HERE.
SHE WAS NO MATCH FOR US.
WE FOUGHT HER FOR YOU.
YOU'LL ALWAYS BE SAFE NOW. SHE CAN'T HURT YOU ANYMORE.
Don't cry, my friends. I'm right here.
Oh, there is sadness in not being able to comfort a friend.

My friends...What trouble I've put them through. If only I could help them with their sorrow.
SNOW WHITE! AT LAST I FOUND YOU. BUT TOO LATE.
It's the prince. He's here.
If he's found me, then let my wish come true that, at last, he and I will have our kiss.

I'VE BEEN LOOKING FOR HER SINCE SHE DISAPPEARED. FROM THE MOMENT I MET HER, IT WAS AS THOUGH A SONG WAS BORN IN MY HEART.
TO SEE YOU HERE, BUT A SHADOW OF HOW BRIGHT YOU WERE IN LIFE--IT BREAKS MY HEART.
My heart wants me to get up. There are so many things for us to do yet.
IF ONLY I COULD WAKE YOU UP SO THAT WE COULD HAVE A GREAT ADVENTURE TOGETHER.
And I have so much to tell you. But at least you've met my dear friends.
ONE LAST GOODBYE TO MY ONE LOVE.
SNOW!
MY FRIENDS. I'VE HAD THE STRANGEST DREAM.

There is so much for us to celebrate after I awoke.
I NEVER STOPPED THINKING OF YOU.
I NEVER STOPPED LOOKING FOR YOU.
To be here, alive, with my friends and my true love.
After all that pain, my greatest wish did come true.
This is my happily ever after.

CECIL CASTELLUCCI

Cecil Castellucci is the award-winning and *New York Times* bestselling author of books and graphic novels for young adults including *Shade, The Changing Girl, Female Furies, Boy Proof, The Plain Janes, Soupy Leaves Home, The Year of the Beasts, Tin Star*, and *Odd Duck*. In 2015, she co-authored *Star Wars Moving Target: A Princess Leia Adventure*. She is currently writing *Batgirl* for DC Comics. Her short stories and short comics have been published in *Strange Horizons*, Tor.com, *Womanthology, Star Trek: Waypoint, Vertigo SFX: Slam!* and many other anthologies. In a former life, she was known as Cecil Seaskull in the nineties indie band, Nerdy Girl. She has written two opera librettos, *Les Aventures de Madame Merveille* (World Premiere in 2010) and *Hockey Noir: The Opera* (World Premiere 2018). She is the former Children's Correspondence Coordinator for *The Rumpus*, a two-time MacDowell Fellow, and the founding YA Editor at the *LA Review of Books*. Cecil lives in Los Angeles, California.

GABRIELE BAGNOLI

Gabriele Bagnoli was born in Verona, Italy, in 1989. He graduated in Communication Sciences. He is a self-taught comics artist. Since 2012, Gabriele has worked as an illustrator for Italian kids' publishing and school publishing. From 2014 to 2017, he worked as inker, colorist, and then as an artist for the comics series *Sacro/Profano*, created by Mirka Andolfo. In 2018, he worked as digital painter for the Italian fantasy comic series *4HOODS*, published by Sergio Bonelli Editore. In 2019, he worked as a comics artist for the French publisher Dupuis (*Ma Jeunesse en BD*) and for the US market with publishers such as BOOM! Studios (*Steven Universe Ongoing*), Dark Horse Comics (*Snow White and the Seven Dwarfs*), and Disney (*Where is Donald?*).

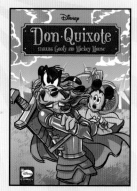

A GRAND ADVENTURE!

From Shuster Award–winning and Eisner–nominated writer Cecil Castellucci, with art by José Pimenta!

CECIL CASTELLUCCI JOSE PIMIENTA

SOUPY LEAVES HOME

"Castellucci has created a strong heroine who both defies conventionality and embodies empowerment."
—KIRKUS REVIEWS

Two misfits with no place to call home take a train-hopping journey from the cold heartbreak of their eastern homes to the sunny promise of California in this Depression-era coming-of-age tale.

ISBN 978-1-61655-431-6 · $14.99

AVAILABLE AT YOUR LOCAL COMICS SHOP OR BOOKSTORE! To find a comics shop in your area, visit comicshoplocator.com. For more information or to order direct: On the web: DarkHorse.com · Email: mailorder@darkhorse.com · Phone: 1-800-862-0052 Mon.–Fri. 9 AM to 5 PM Pacific Time